All About Me

MY DAY

Morning, Noon, and Night

Written by Lisa Bullard • Illustrated by Brandon Reibeling

Content Advisor: Lorraine O. Moore, Ph.D., Educational Psychologist
Reading Advisor: Lauren A. Liang, M.A.
Literacy Education, University of Minnesota, Minneapolis, Minnesota

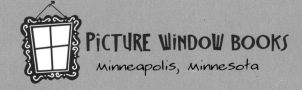

PICTURE WINDOW BOOKS
Minneapolis, Minnesota

For My Sam—L.B.

Designer: Melissa Voda
Page production: Picture Window Books
The illustrations in this book were prepared digitally.

Picture Window Books
5115 Excelsior Boulevard, Suite 232
Minneapolis, MN 55416
1-877-845-8392
www.picturewindowbooks.com

Printed in the United States of America.

Library of Congress Cataloging-in-Publication Data
Bullard, Lisa.
   My day : morning, noon, and night / written by Lisa Bullard;
   illustrated by Brandon Reibeling.
      p. cm. — (All about me)
   Summary: Sam spends a typical day having breakfast with his family,
learning and having fun at school, playing with his friend Max, and heading
for bed with his dog, Lucky.
   ISBN 1-4048-0159-6 (paperback)
   ISBN 1-4048-0045-X (hardcover)
   [1. Day-Fiction. 2. Family life-Fiction. 3. Schools-Fiction. 4. Friendship-Fiction.]
I. Reibeling, Brandon, ill. II. Title.
   PZ7.B91245 My 2003
   [Fic]-dc21
                                                                    2002008547

My dog, Lucky, wakes me up by licking my face. That's how he says, "Good morning, Sam!" This is how I start my day.

3

Mom says dog baths don't count, so I wash my face in the sink and comb my hair.

I like wearing the shirt from my favorite pizza place. But if there's pizza sauce spilled on it, Mom sends me back to put on clean clothes.

We all help with breakfast. I set the table. My brothers pour the cereal and juice. Dad's in charge of the toast, but sometimes he forgets. Lucky likes burned-toast days.

After breakfast, everyone is in a hurry. Dad says there is always enough time to brush our teeth.

My brothers walk to their school.
I meet my best friend, Max,
at the bus stop. When the
school bus comes, we race
for the back seat.

At school, we learn important
stuff about dinosaurs and mummies
and spaceships and sharks.
Sometimes we do projects.

It's fun when we get to make
a mess with clay in art
or play kickball in gym.

At noon, the noisiest place at school is the lunchroom. I trade my cookies for Max's chips. He trades his peanut butter for my grilled cheese.

After lunch, we go outside for recess. Max and I like to play on the monkey bars.

13

After school, we take the bus
to Max's house. His mom is home,
but my mom is still at work.
Max and I ride bikes, or dig
in the dirt, or throw a football.

Dad picks me up on his way home
from work. He always asks me what
I learned since breakfast. Mom picks
up my brothers from soccer practice.

We have two rules at dinnertime.
One is "No talking with your
mouth full."

The other is "Eat all your vegetables
before you leave the table."

At night, when dinner is cleaned up, it's time for homework.

After I study, I play games with my brothers or read a book. Some nights we watch TV.

Bedtime always comes too early. Most nights I take a bath. When I've washed up and brushed my teeth, Mom and Dad tuck me into bed.

My room is quiet. Lucky is warm on my feet. When I wake up tomorrow, it will be my day all over again.

Activity #1: Telling Time

Look back through the story. Find the answers to these questions in the pictures:

What time does Sam wake up in the morning?

What time does he eat breakfast?

What time does he go to school?

What time does he eat lunch?

What time does he play at Max's house?

What time does he do his homework?

What time does he go to bed?

22

Activity #2: Making a Picture Journal of Your Day

1. Take three or more sheets of paper and stack them neatly. Fold the stack in half.

2. Staple several times along the folded edge. You've made a blank book.

3. Think about your own day. What happens in the morning? What happens in the afternoon? What happens at night?

4. Use each page to draw a picture of something you do during the day. The first page of your book should show the very first thing you do in the morning. The last page should show the last thing you do each night.

5. When you are done telling the story of your day, decorate the cover of your book and give it a name. Then think about Sam's day. How is his day different from yours? How is it the same?

Words to Know

art—a class at school in which you paint, make clay pots, and do other creative projects

gym—a class at school in which you exercise and play active games

homework—school assignments that your teacher asks you to do at home

lunchroom—the place where you eat lunch at school, also called the cafeteria

noon—12:00 P.M., the middle of the day

recess—a time during the school day just for playing

To Learn More

At the Library

Ballard, Robin. My Day, Your Day. New York: Greenwillow Books, 2001.
Foster, John, editor. Around the Day. Oxford: Oxford University Press, 2000.
Uff, Caroline. Lulu's Busy Day. New York: Walker, 2000.

On the Web

KidsHealth: For information on you and your health
    http://www.kidshealth.org/kid

Sesame Workshop: Play games and explore the world.
    http://www.sesameworkshop.com

Want to learn more about what makes you you?
    Visit FACT HOUND at http://www.facthound.com.